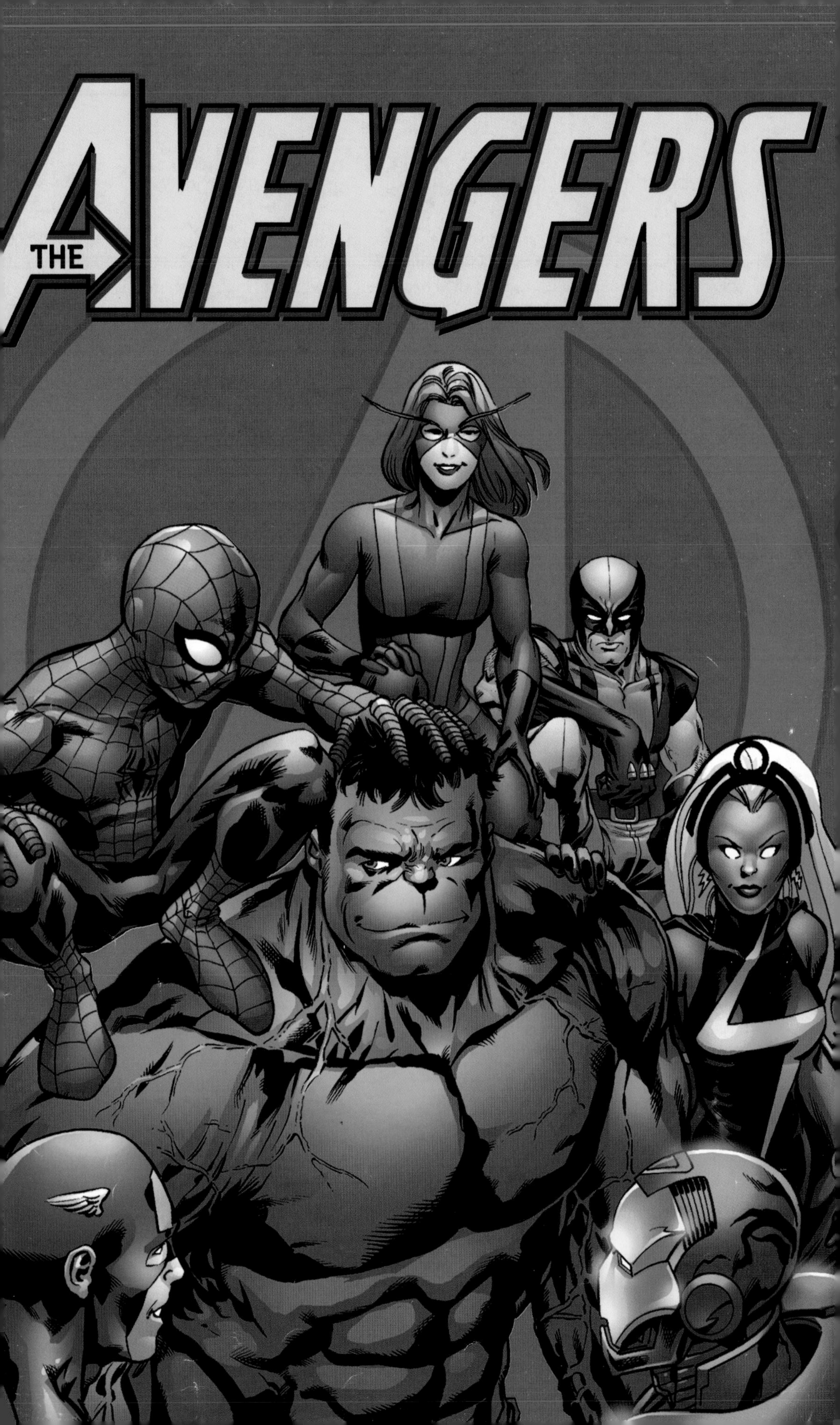
THE
AVENGERS

VISIT US AT
www.abdopublishing.com

Reinforced library bound edition published in 2011 by Spotlight, a division of the ABDO Group, 8000
West 78th Street, Edina, Minnesota 55439. Spotlight produces high-quality reinforced library bound
editions for schools and libraries. Published by agreement with Marvel Characters, Inc.

Printed in the United States of America, Melrose Park, Illinois.
042010
092010
 This book contains at least 10% recycled material.

Library of Congress Cataloging-in-Publication Data

Tobin, Paul.
 Which wish? / story, Paul Tobin ; art, Jacopo Camagni.
    p. cm. -- (The Avengers)
 "Marvel."
 ISBN 978-1-59961-769-5
 1. Graphic novels. I. Camagni, Jacopo, ill. II. Avengers (Comic strip) III. Title.
 PZ7.7.T62Whi 2010
 741.5'973--dc22
                            2009052835

All Spotlight books have reinforced library bindings and
are manufactured in the United States of America.

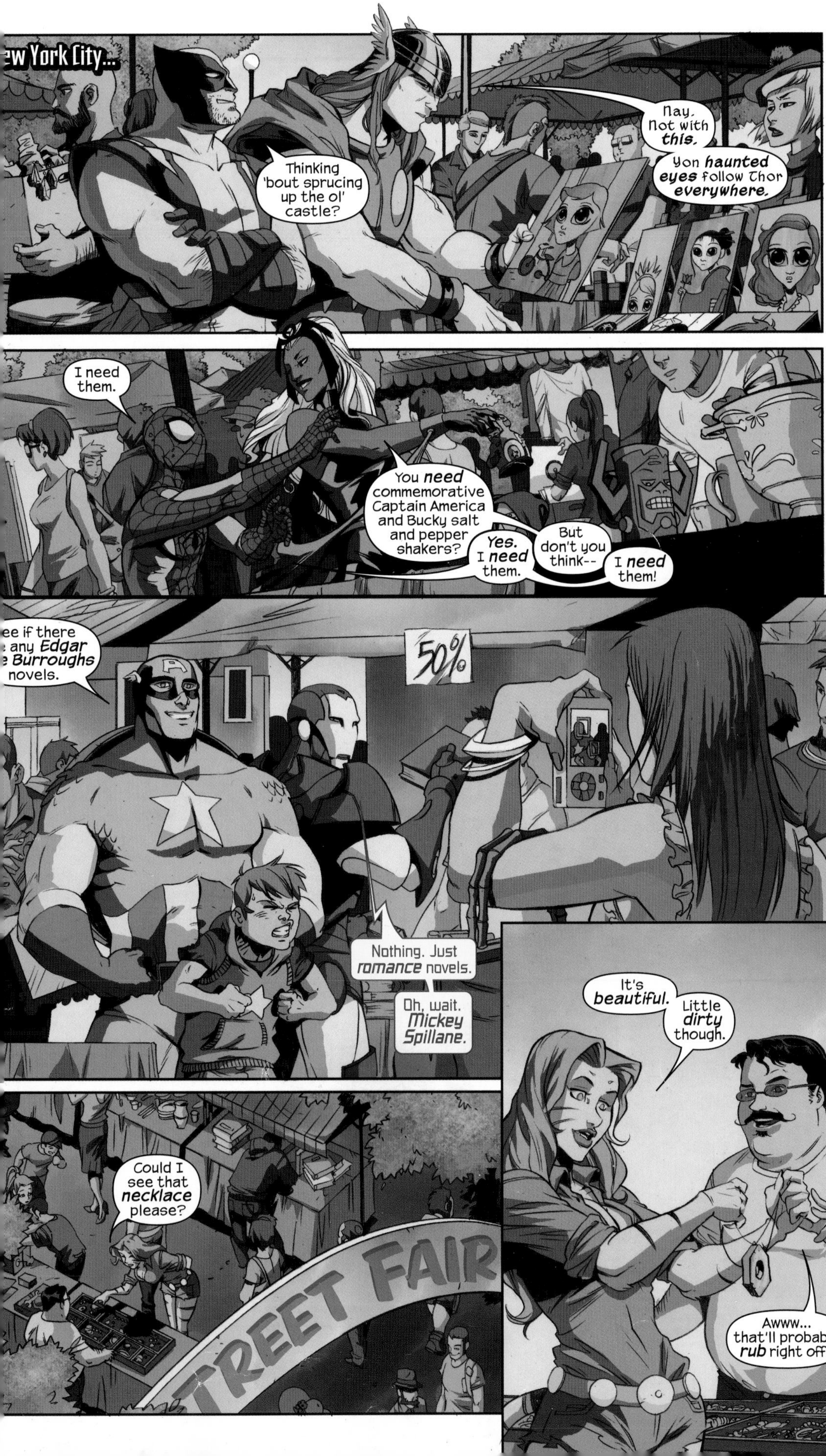
ew York City...
Thinking 'bout sprucing up the ol' castle?
Nay. Not with this.
Yon haunted eyes follow Thor everywhere.
I need them.
You need commemorative Captain America and Bucky salt and pepper shakers?
Yes. I need them.
But don't you think--
I need them!
ee if there any Edgar Burroughs novels.
50%
Nothing. Just romance novels.
Oh, wait. Mickey Spillane.
Could I see that necklace please?
STREET FAIR
It's beautiful.
Little dirty though.
Awww... that'll probably rub right off.

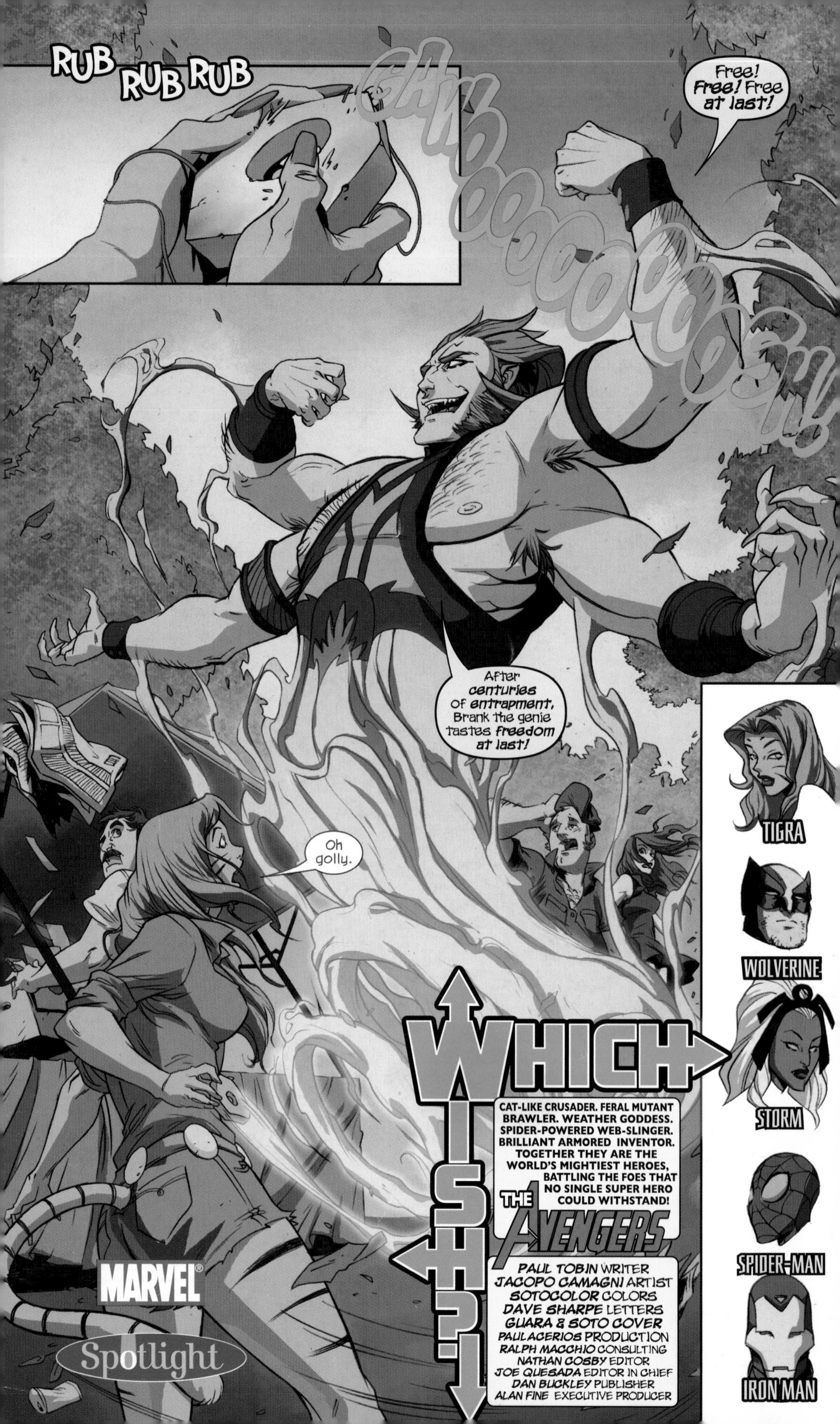

RUB RUB RUB
CHWOOOOOOOOOOOSH!
Free! Free! Free at last!
After centuries of entrapment, Brank the genie tastes freedom at last!
Oh golly.
TIGRA
WOLVERINE
STORM
SPIDER-MAN
IRON MAN
WHICH WISH?!
CAT-LIKE CRUSADER. FERAL MUTANT BRAWLER. WEATHER GODDESS. SPIDER-POWERED WEB-SLINGER. BRILLIANT ARMORED INVENTOR. TOGETHER THEY ARE THE WORLD'S MIGHTIEST HEROES, BATTLING THE FOES THAT NO SINGLE SUPER HERO COULD WITHSTAND!
THE AVENGERS
PAUL TOBIN WRITER
JACOPO CAMAGNI ARTIST
SOTOCOLOR COLORS
DAVE SHARPE LETTERS
GUARA & SOTO COVER
PAUL ACERIOS PRODUCTION
RALPH MACCHIO CONSULTING
NATHAN COSBY EDITOR
JOE QUESADA EDITOR IN CHIEF
DAN BUCKLEY PUBLISHER
ALAN FINE EXECUTIVE PRODUCER
MARVEL®
Spotlight

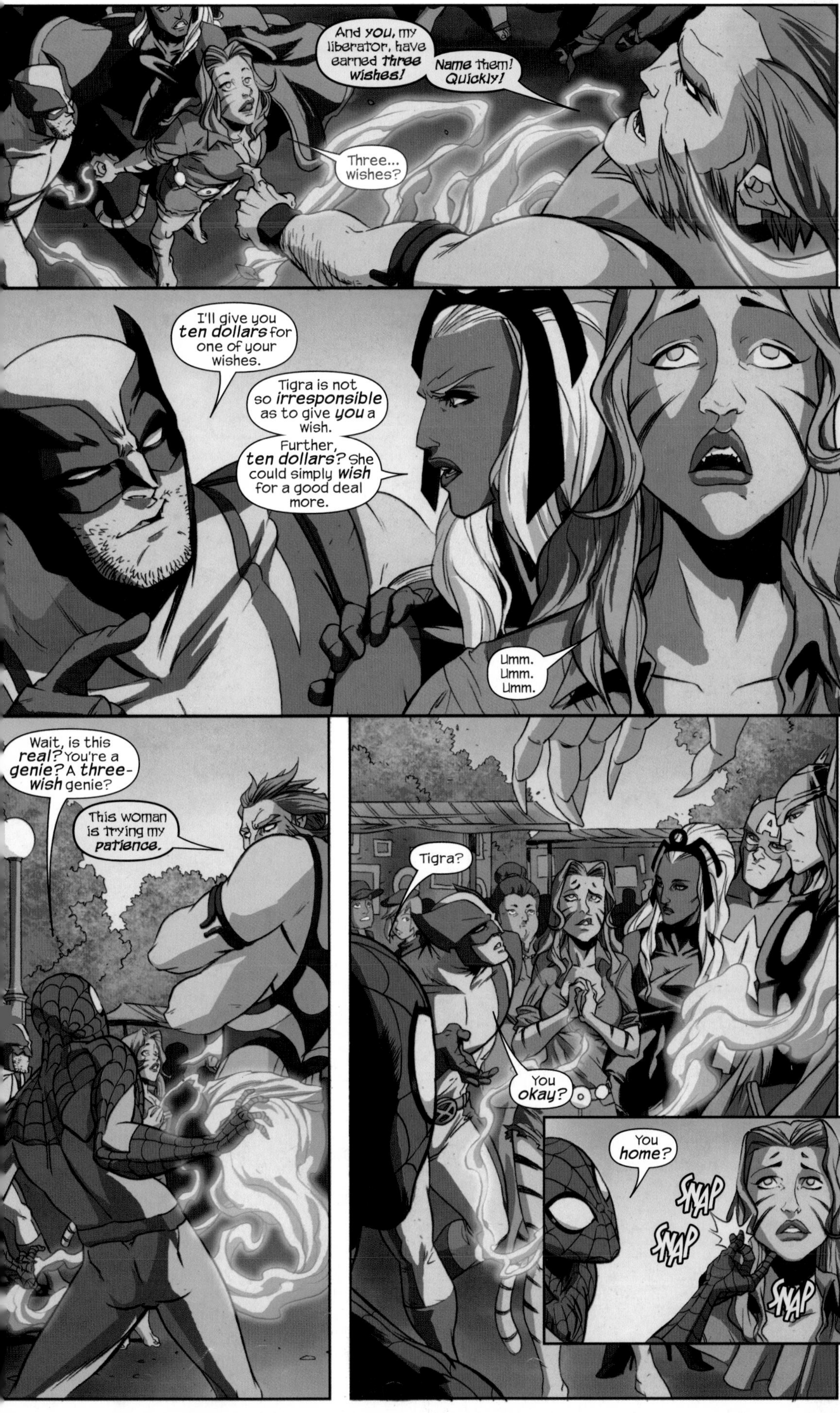

And you, my liberator, have earned three wishes!
Name them! Quickly!
Three... wishes?
I'll give you ten dollars for one of your wishes.
Tigra is not so irresponsible as to give you a wish.
Further, ten dollars? She could simply wish for a good deal more.
Umm. Umm. Umm.
Wait, is this real? You're a genie? A three-wish genie?
This woman is trying my patience.
Tigra?
You okay?
You home?
SNAP
SNAP
SNAP

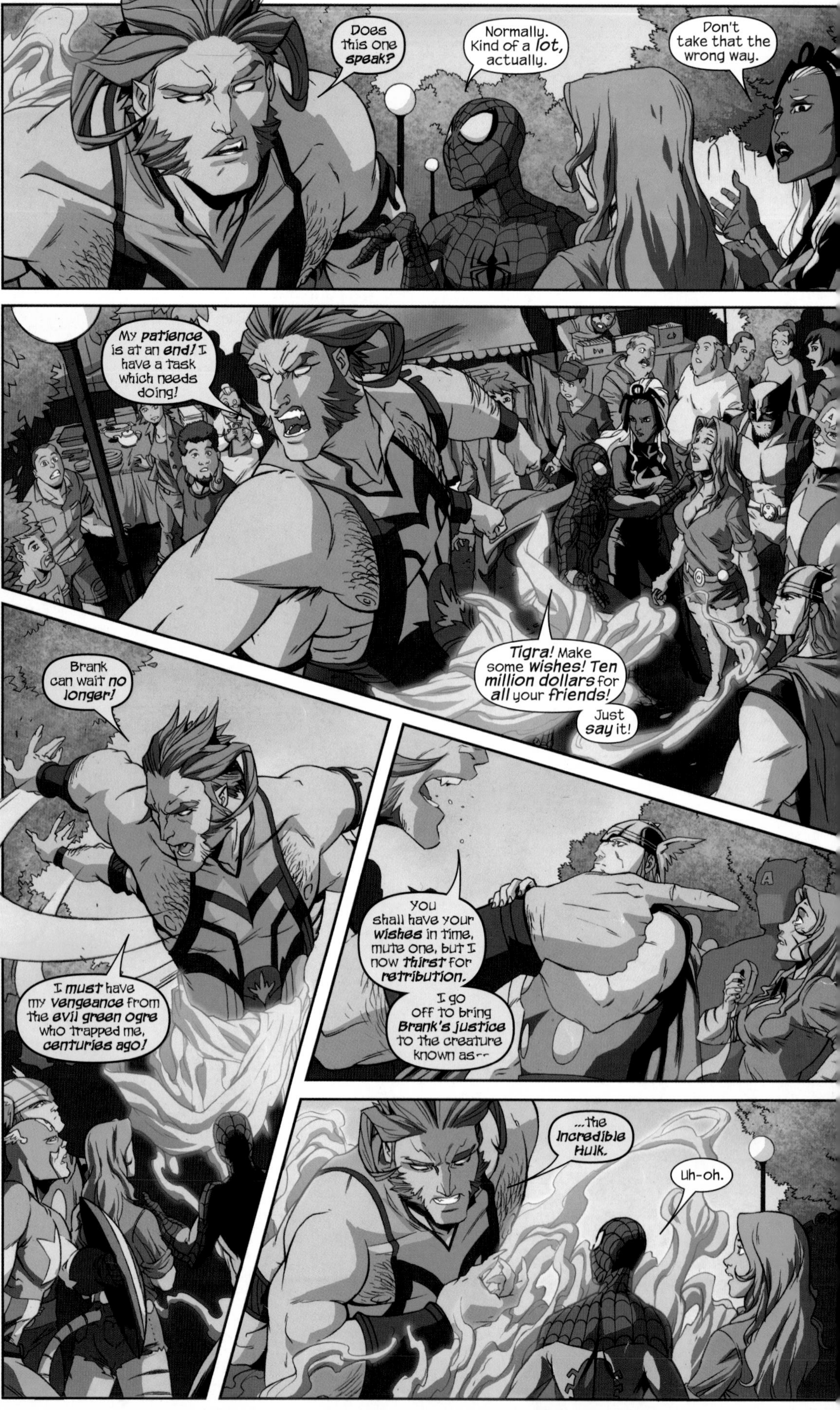

Does this one speak?
Normally. Kind of a lot, actually.
Don't take that the wrong way.
My patience is at an end! I have a task which needs doing!
Tigra! Make some wishes! Ten million dollars for all your friends!
Just say it!
Brank can wait no longer!
I must have my vengeance from the evil green ogre who trapped me, centuries ago!
You shall have your wishes in time, mute one, but I now thirst for retribution.
I go off to bring Brank's justice to the creature known as--
...the Incredible Hulk.
Uh-oh.

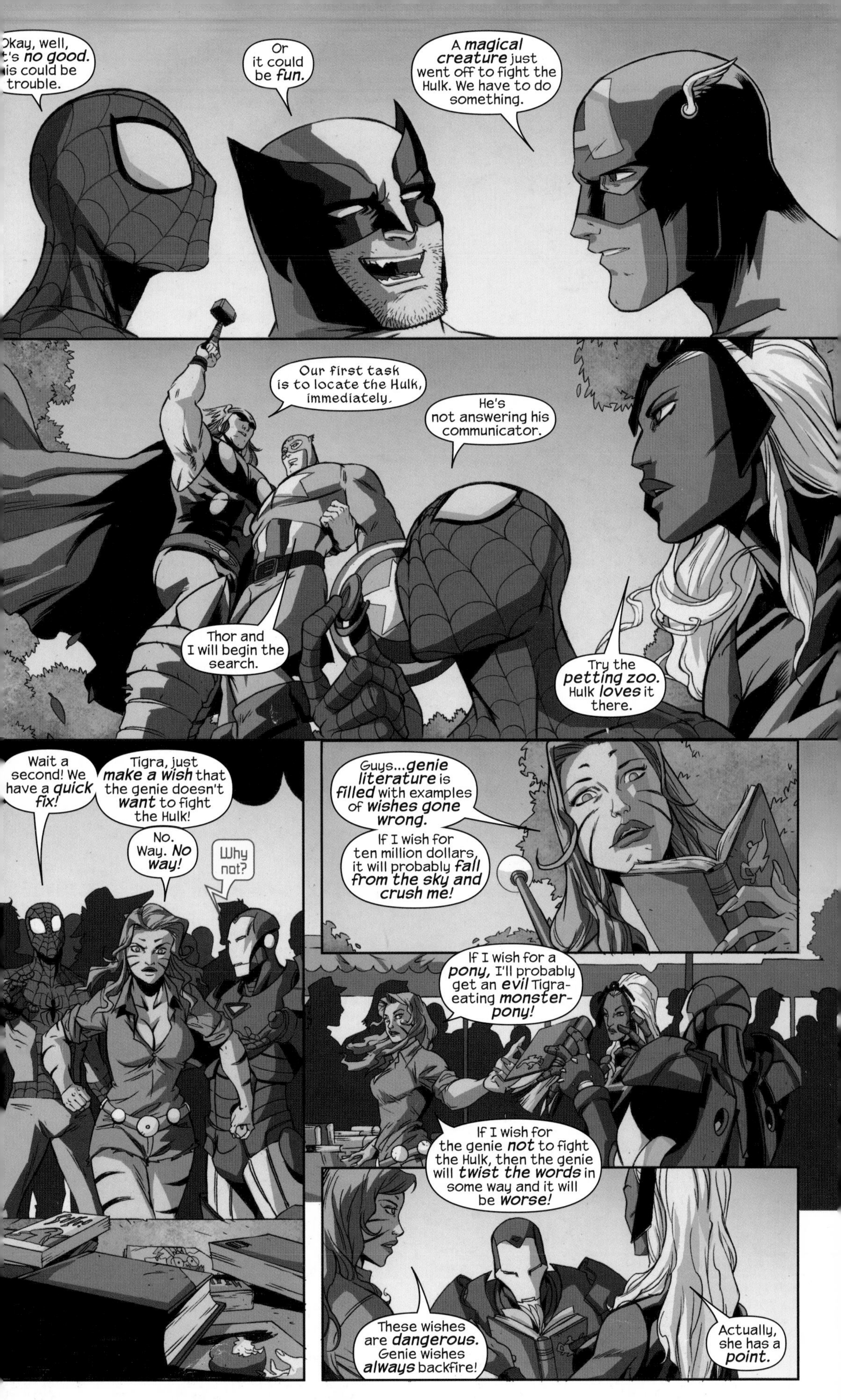
Okay, well, it's no good. This could be trouble.
Or it could be fun.
A magical creature just went off to fight the Hulk. We have to do something.
Our first task is to locate the Hulk, immediately.
He's not answering his communicator.
Thor and I will begin the search.
Try the petting zoo. Hulk loves it there.
Wait a second! We have a quick fix!
Tigra, just make a wish that the genie doesn't want to fight the Hulk!
No. Way. No way!
Why not?
Guys...genie literature is filled with examples of wishes gone wrong.
If I wish for ten million dollars, it will probably fall from the sky and crush me!
If I wish for a pony, I'll probably get an evil Tigra-eating monster-pony!
If I wish for the genie not to fight the Hulk, then the genie will twist the words in some way and it will be worse!
These wishes are dangerous. Genie wishes always backfire!
Actually, she has a point.

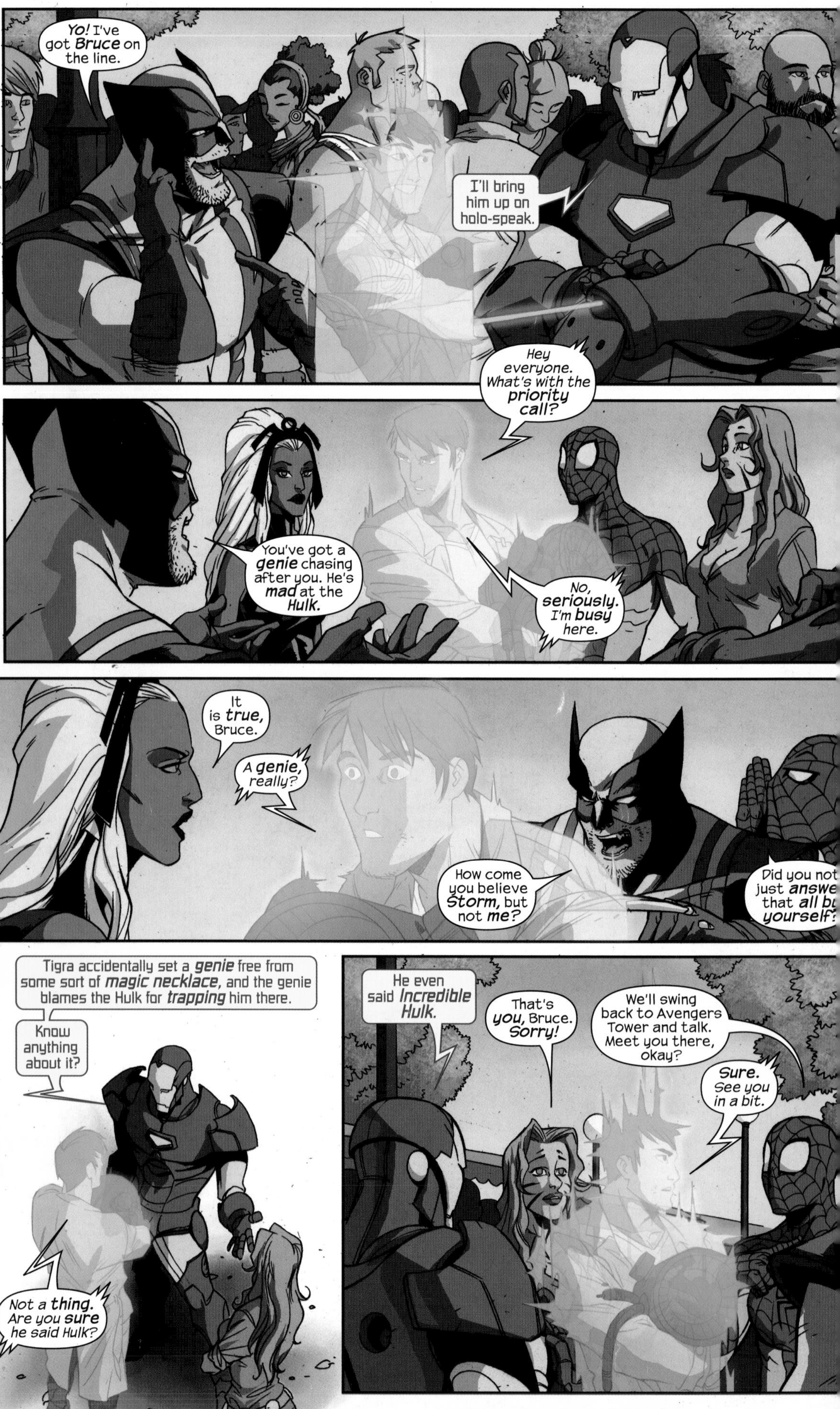

Yo! I've got Bruce on the line.
I'll bring him up on holo-speak.
Hey everyone. What's with the priority call?
You've got a genie chasing after you. He's mad at the Hulk.
No, seriously. I'm busy here.
It is true, Bruce.
A genie, really?
How come you believe Storm, but not me?
Did you not just answe that all b yourself?
Tigra accidentally set a genie free from some sort of magic necklace, and the genie blames the Hulk for trapping him there.
Know anything about it?
Not a thing. Are you sure he said Hulk?
He even said Incredible Hulk.
That's you, Bruce. Sorry!
We'll swing back to Avengers Tower and talk. Meet you there, okay?
Sure. See you in a bit.

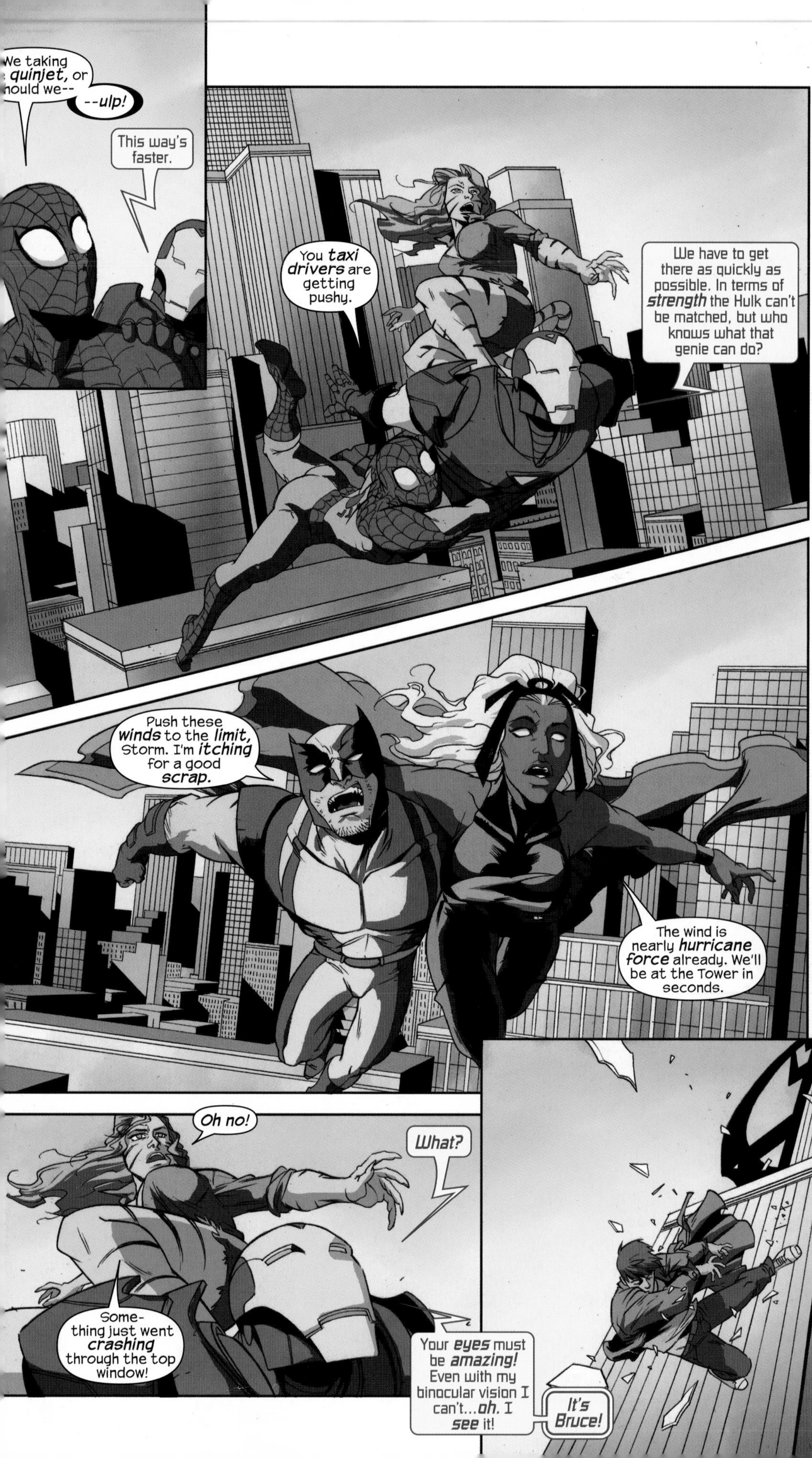
We taking quinjet, or hould we--
--ulp!
This way's faster.
You taxi drivers are getting pushy.
We have to get there as quickly as possible. In terms of strength the Hulk can't be matched, but who knows what that genie can do?
Push these winds to the limit, Storm. I'm itching for a good scrap.
The wind is nearly hurricane force already. We'll be at the Tower in seconds.
Oh no!
What?
Something just went crashing through the top window!
Your eyes must be amazing! Even with my binocular vision I can't...oh. I see it!
It's Bruce!

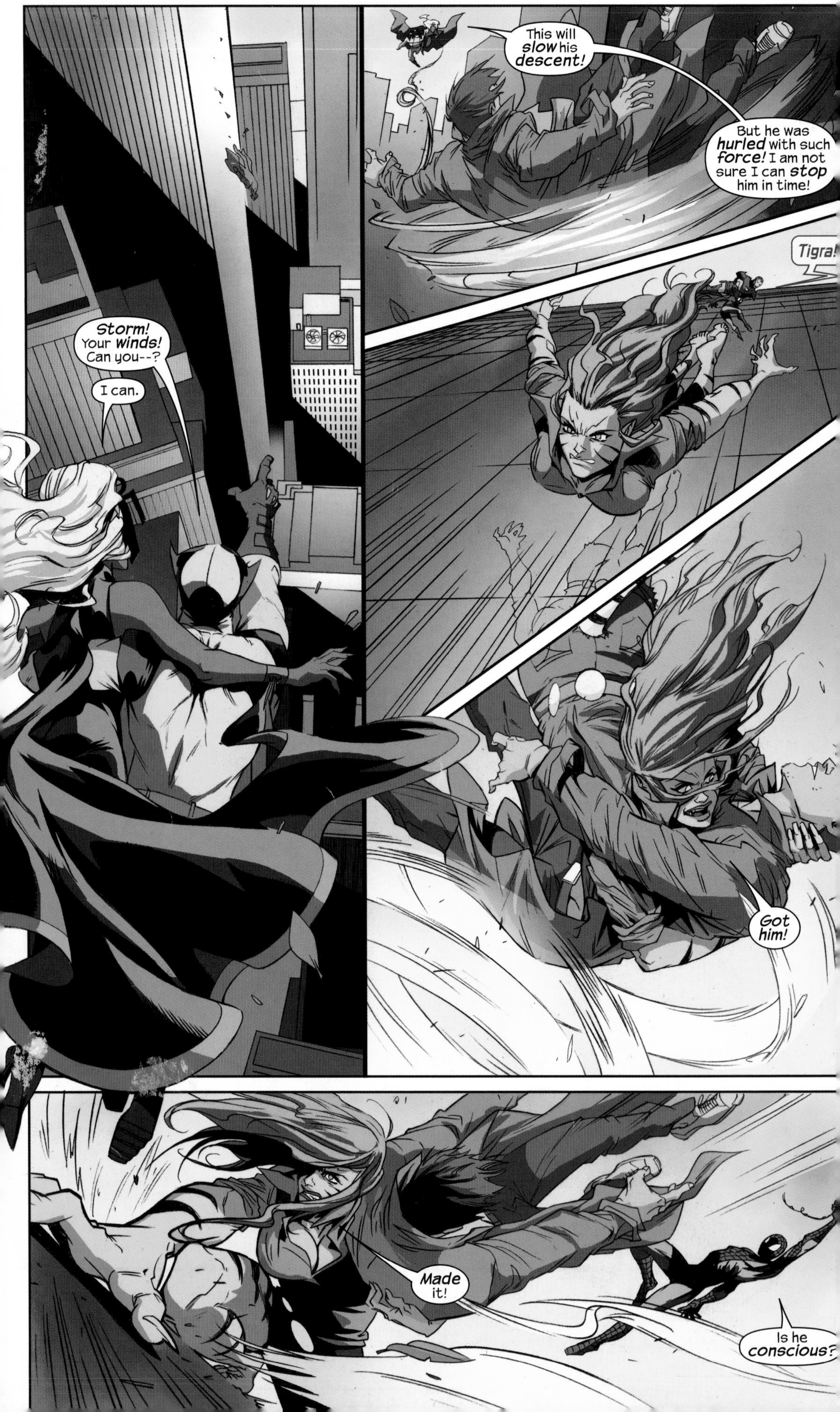
Storm! Your winds! Can you--?
I can.
This will slow his descent!
But he was hurled with such force! I am not sure I can stop him in time!
Tigra!
Got him!
Made it!
Is he conscious?

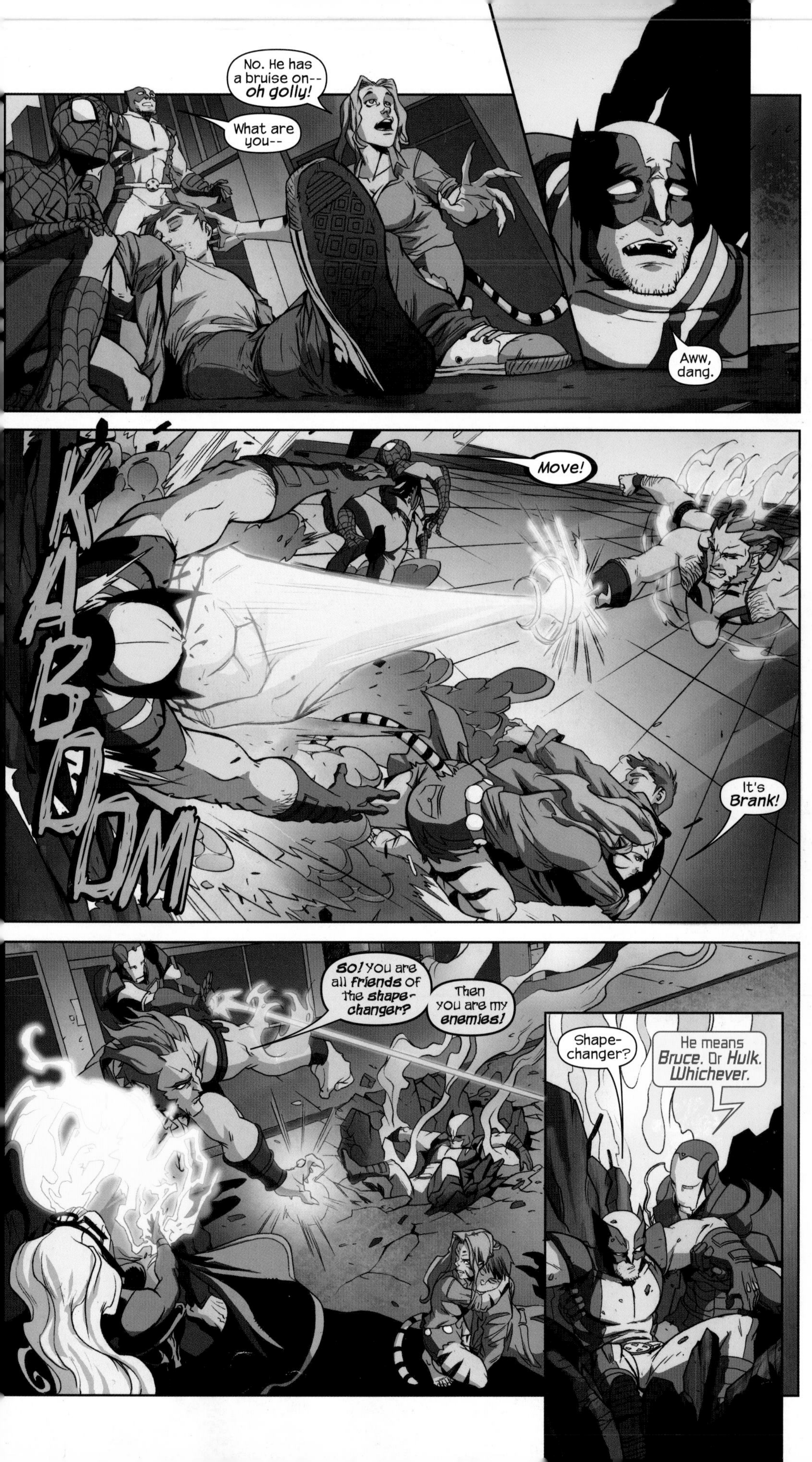
No. He has a bruise on-- oh golly!
What are you--
Aww, dang.
KABOOM
Move!
It's Brank!
So! You are all friends of the shape-changer?
Then you are my enemies!
Shape-changer?
He means Bruce. Or Hulk. Whichever.

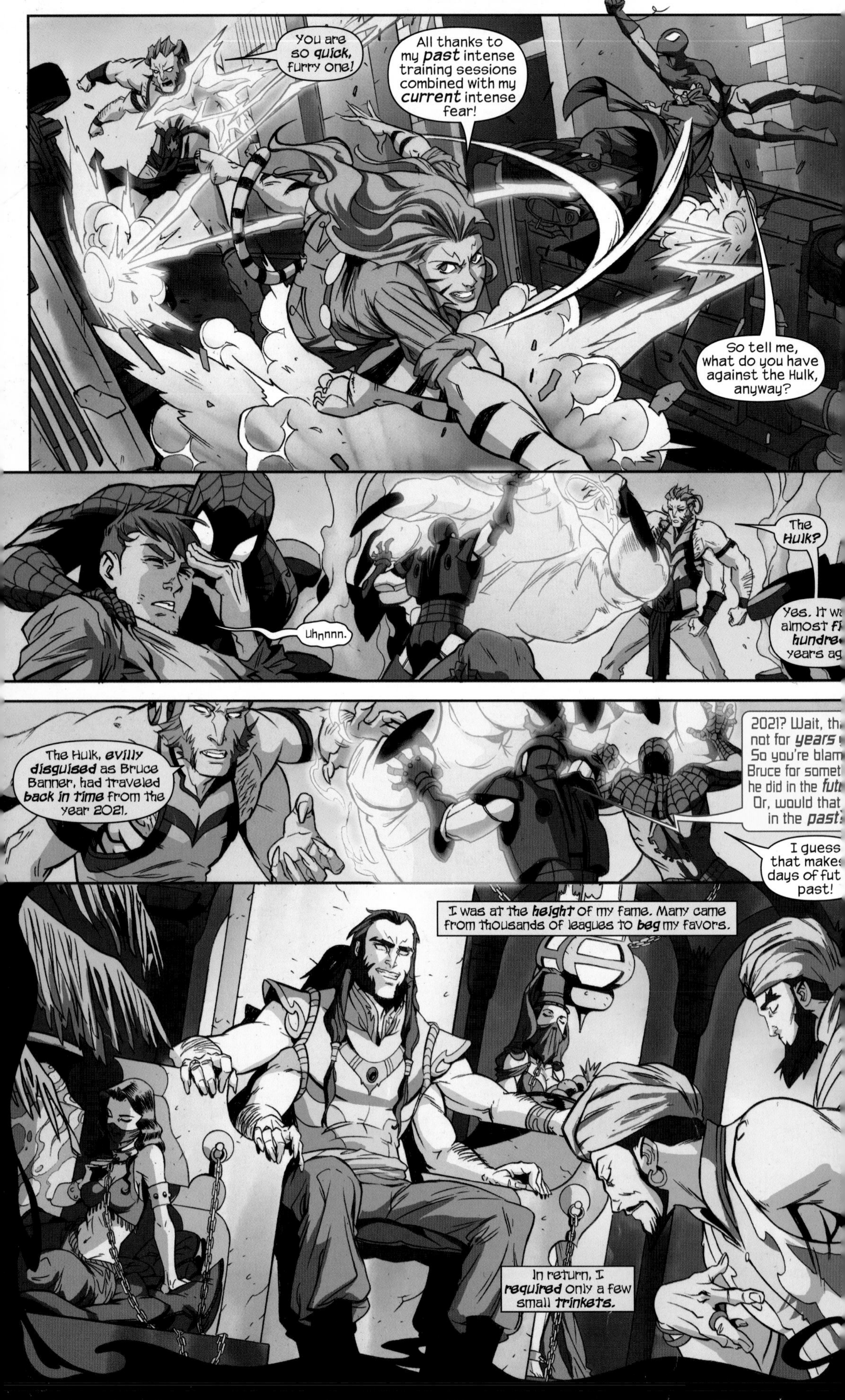

You are so quick, furry one!
All thanks to my past intense training sessions combined with my current intense fear!
So tell me, what do you have against the Hulk, anyway?
Uhnnnn.
The Hulk?
Yes. It wa almost fi hundre years ag
The Hulk, evilly disguised as Bruce Banner, had traveled back in time from the year 2021.
2021? Wait, th not for years So you're blam Bruce for somet he did in the futu Or, would that in the past
I guess that makes days of fut past!
I was at the height of my fame. Many came from thousands of leagues to beg my favors.
In return, I required only a few small trinkets.

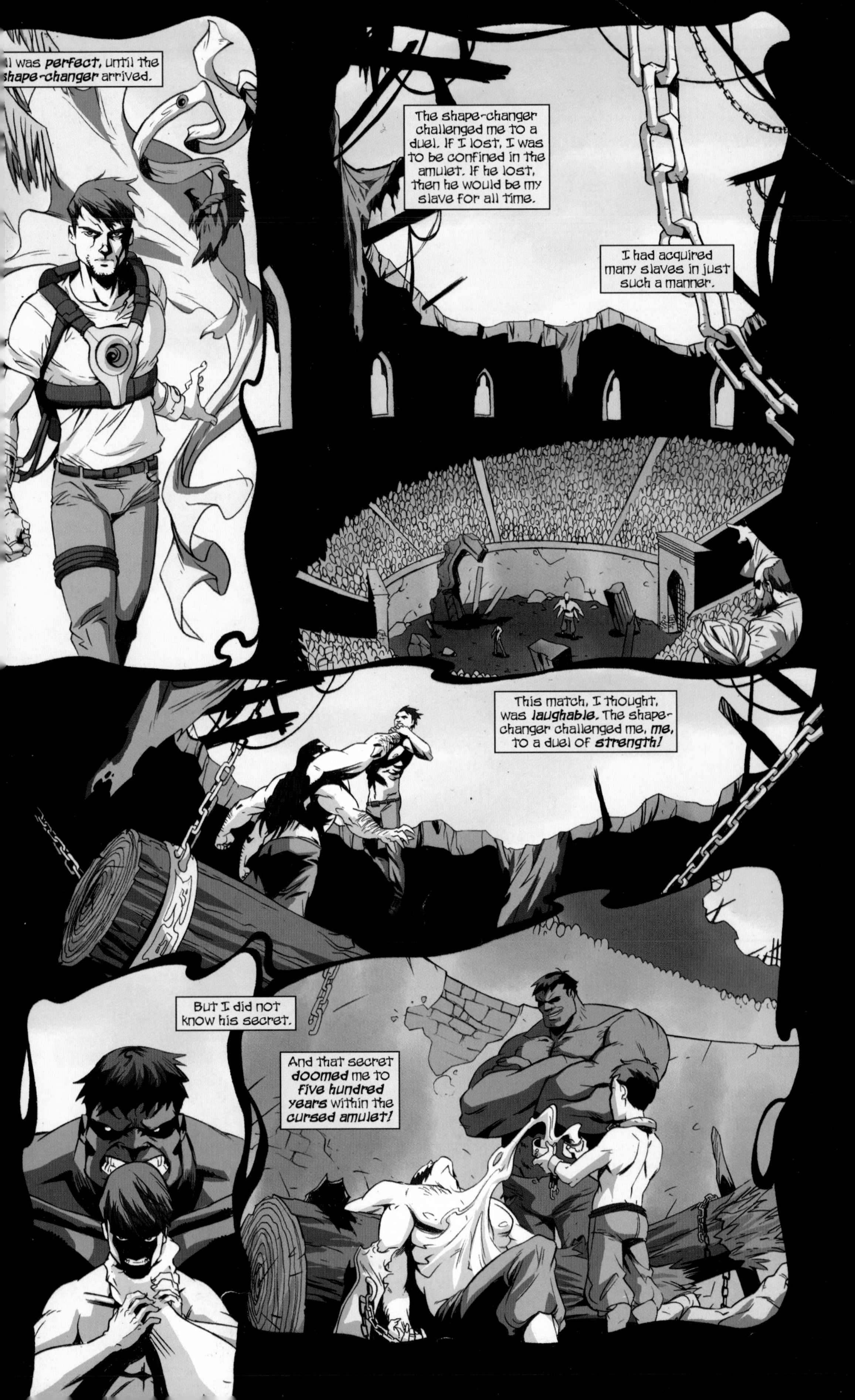
ll was perfect, until the shape-changer arrived.
The shape-changer challenged me to a duel. If I lost, I was to be confined in the amulet. If he lost, then he would be my slave for all time.
I had acquired many slaves in just such a manner.
This match, I thought, was laughable. The shape-changer challenged me, me, to a duel of strength!
But I did not know his secret.
And that secret doomed me to five hundred years within the cursed amulet!

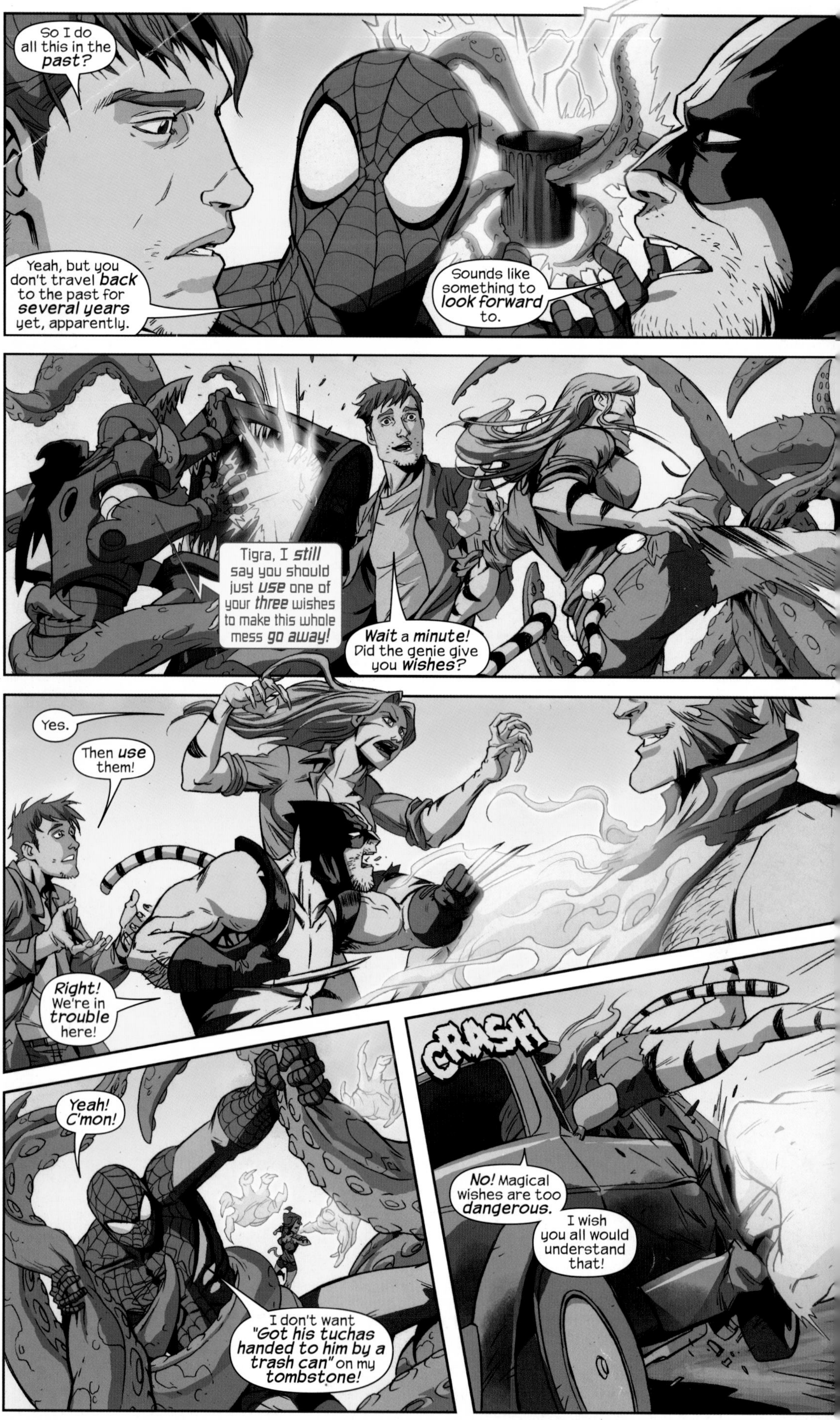
So I do all this in the *past?*
Yeah, but you don't travel *back* to the past for *several years* yet, apparently.
Sounds like something to *look forward* to.
Tigra, I *still* say you should just *use* one of your *three* wishes to make this whole mess *go away!*
Wait a *minute!* Did the genie give you *wishes?*
Yes.
Then *use* them!
Right! We're in *trouble* here!
Yeah! C'mon!
I don't want *"Got his tuchas handed to him by a trash can"* on my *tombstone!*
CRASH
No! Magical wishes are too *dangerous.*
I wish you all would understand that!

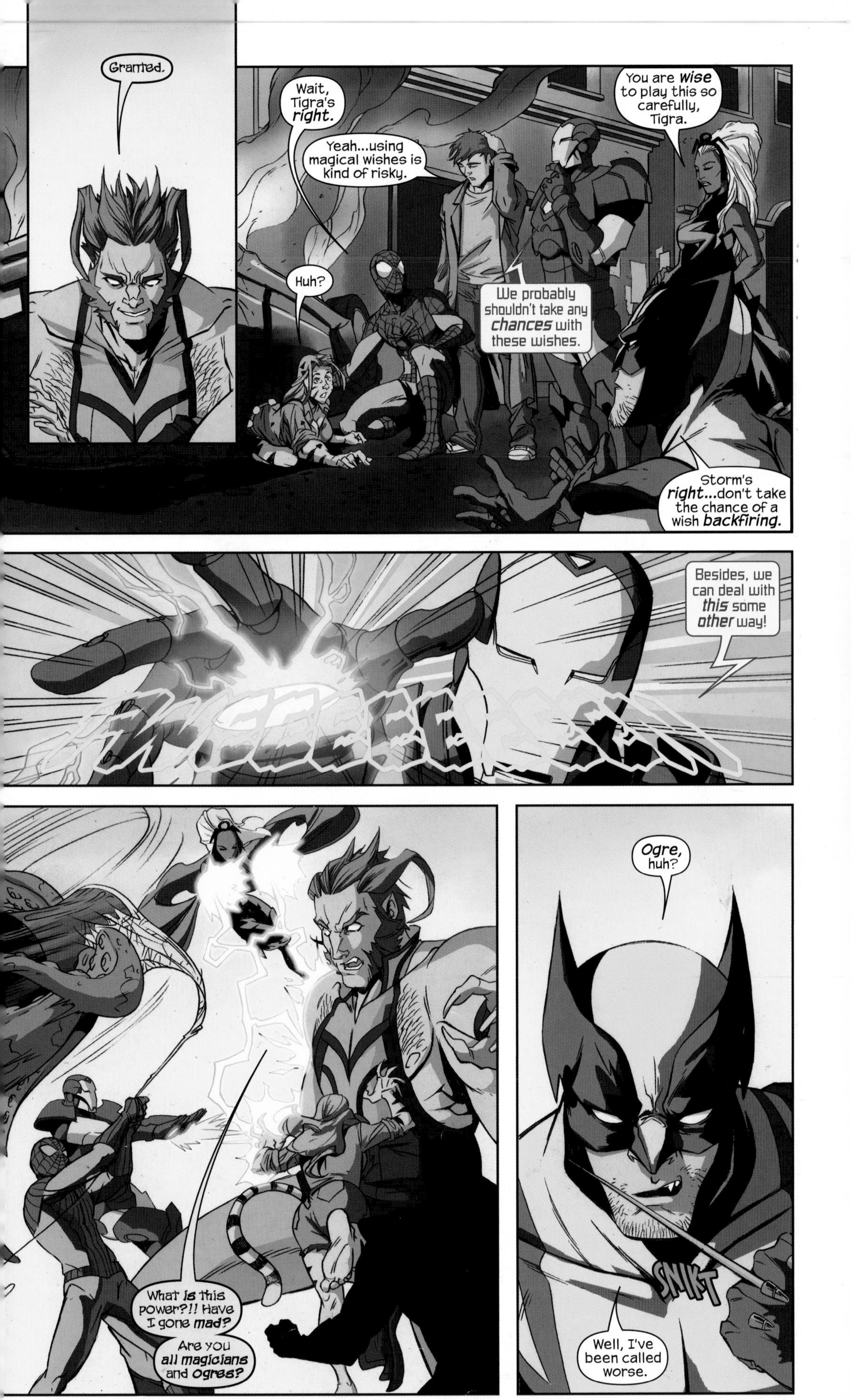
Granted.
Wait, Tigra's right.
Yeah...using magical wishes is kind of risky.
You are wise to play this so carefully, Tigra.
Huh?
We probably shouldn't take any chances with these wishes.
Storm's right...don't take the chance of a wish backfiring.
Besides, we can deal with this some other way!
What is this power?!! Have I gone mad?
Are you all magicians and ogres?
Ogre, huh?
SNIKT
Well, I've been called worse.

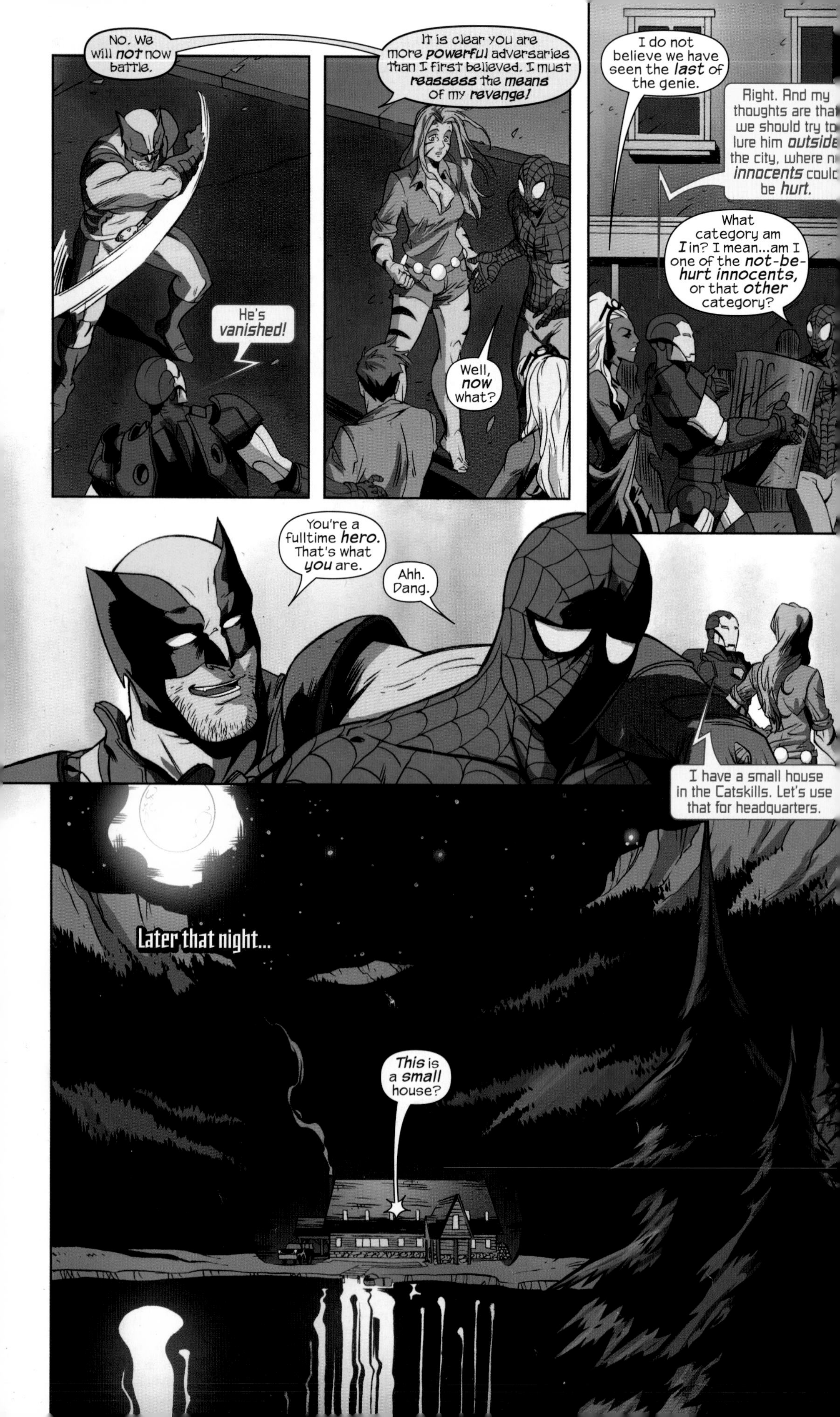

No. We will not now battle.
It is clear you are more powerful adversaries than I first believed. I must reassess the means of my revenge!
He's vanished!
Well, now what?
I do not believe we have seen the last of the genie.
Right. And my thoughts are that we should try to lure him outside the city, where no innocents could be hurt.
What category am I in? I mean...am I one of the not-be-hurt innocents, or that other category?
You're a fulltime hero. That's what you are.
Ahh. Dang.
I have a small house in the Catskills. Let's use that for headquarters.
Later that night...
This is a small house?

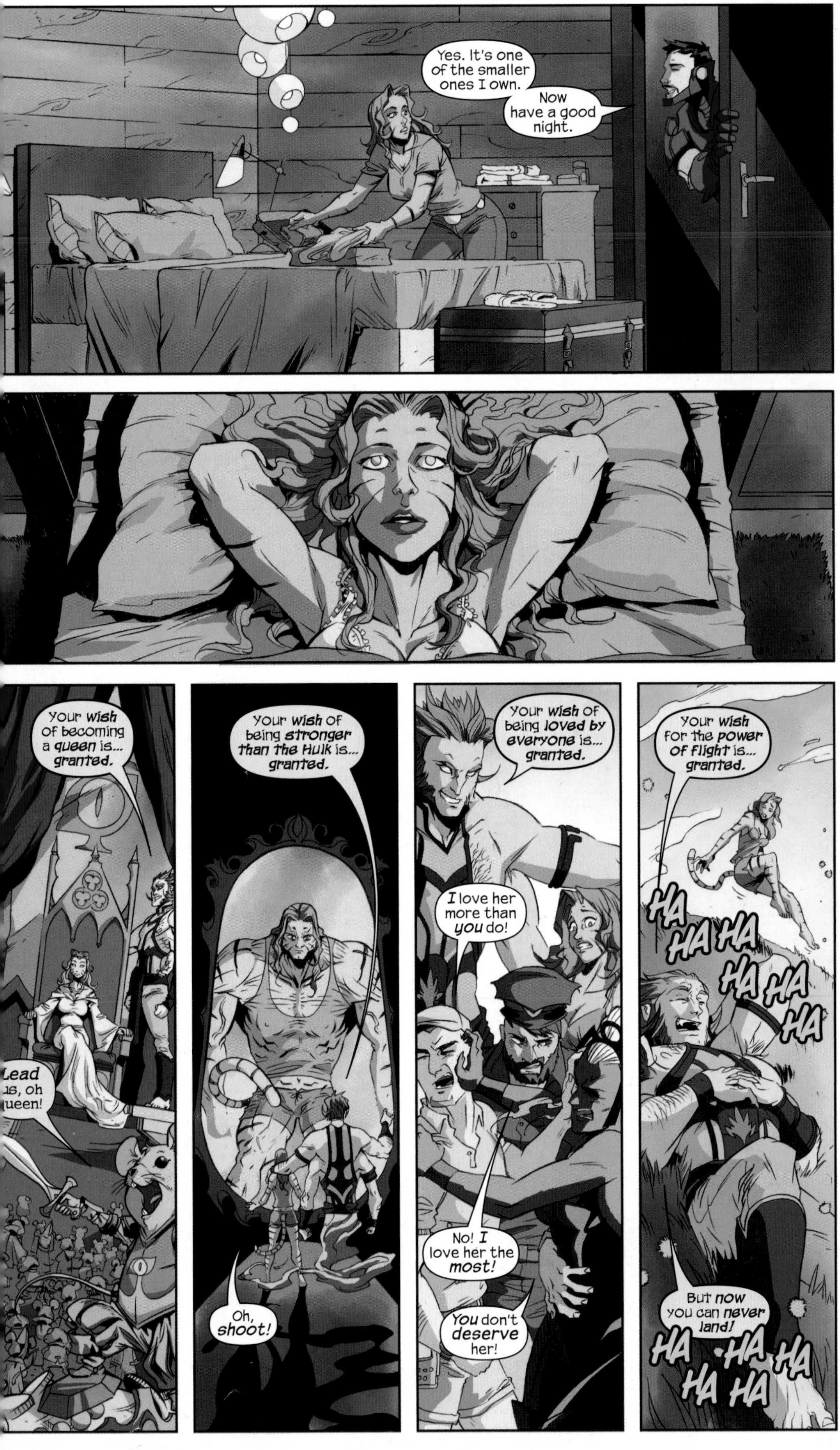

Yes. It's one of the smaller ones I own.
Now have a good night.
Your wish of becoming a queen is... granted.
Lead us, oh queen!
Your wish of being stronger than the Hulk is... granted.
Oh, shoot!
Your wish of being loved by everyone is... granted.
I love her more than you do!
No! I love her the most!
You don't deserve her!
Your wish for the power of flight is... granted.
HA HA HA HA HA HA HA
But now you can never land!
HA HA HA HA HA HA

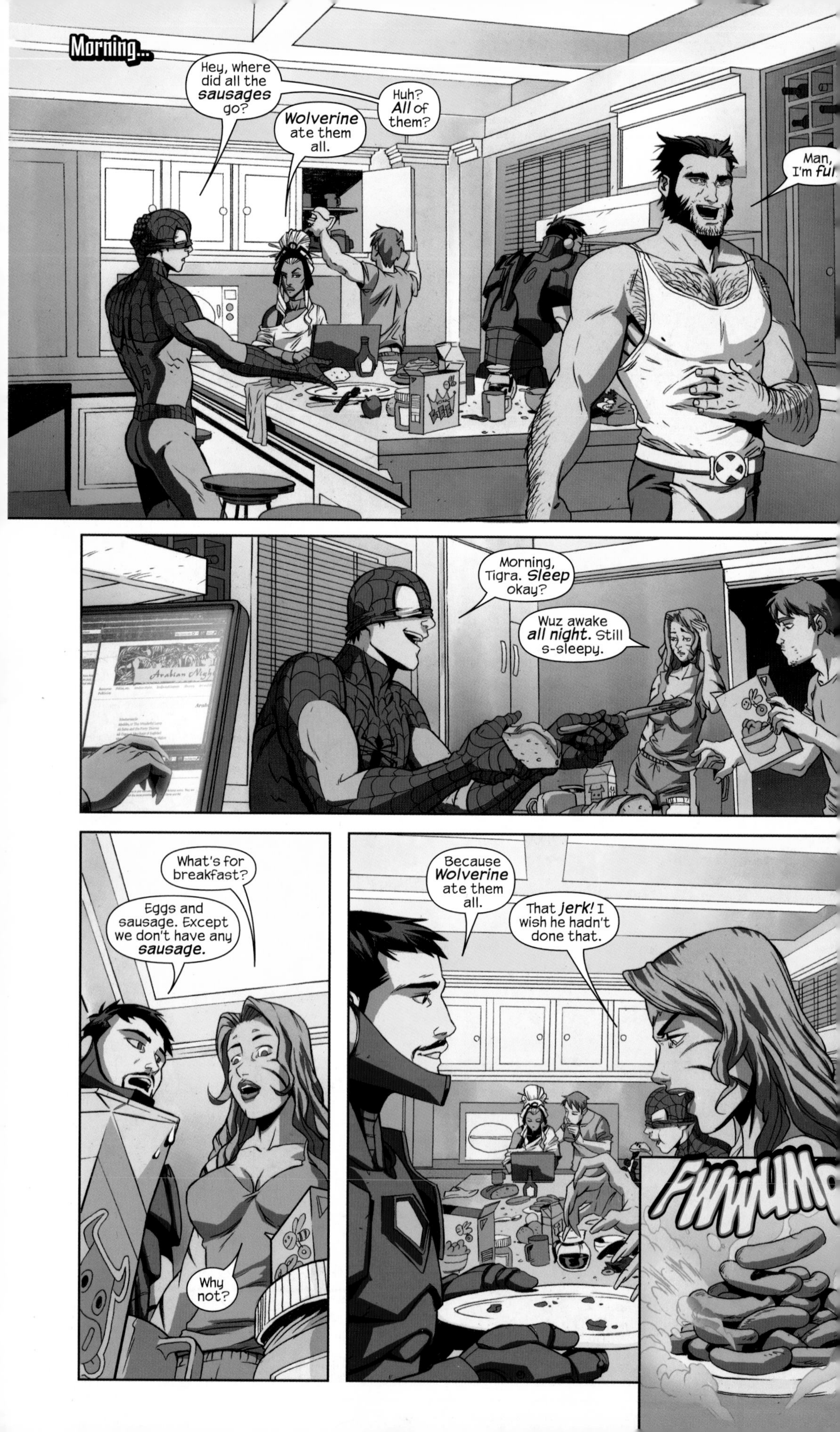

Morning...
Hey, where did all the sausages go?
Huh? All of them?
Wolverine ate them all.
Man, I'm ful
Morning, Tigra. Sleep okay?
Wuz awake all night. Still s-sleepy.
What's for breakfast?
Eggs and sausage. Except we don't have any sausage.
Why not?
Because Wolverine ate them all.
That jerk! I wish he hadn't done that.
FWWUMP

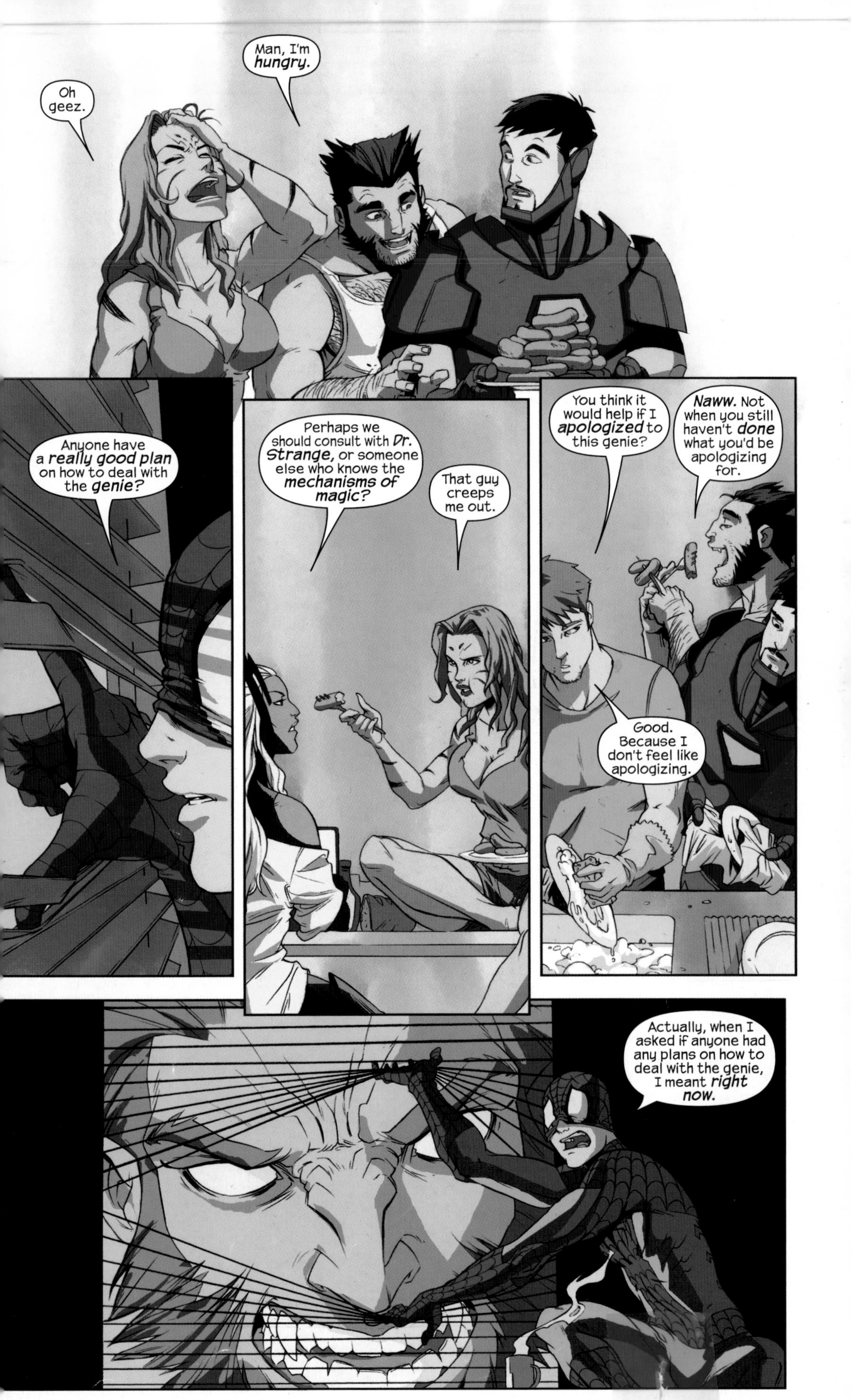
Oh geez.
Man, I'm *hungry.*
Anyone have a *really good plan* on how to deal with the *genie?*
Perhaps we should consult with *Dr. Strange,* or someone else who knows the *mechanisms of magic?*
That guy creeps me out.
You think it would help if I *apologized* to this genie?
Naww. Not when you still haven't *done* what you'd be apologizing for.
Good. Because I don't feel like apologizing.
Actually, when I asked if anyone had any plans on how to deal with the genie, I meant *right now.*

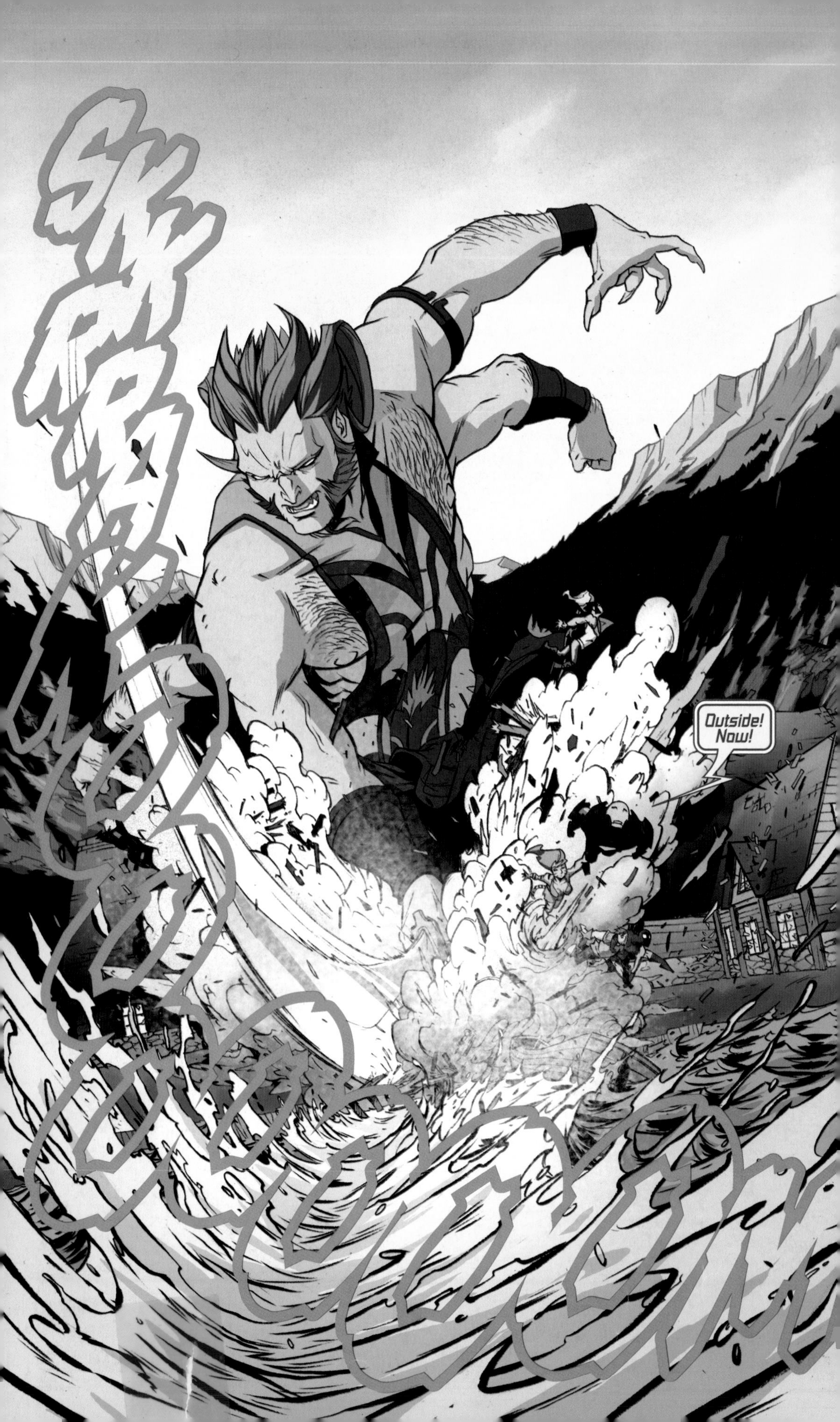
Outside! Now!

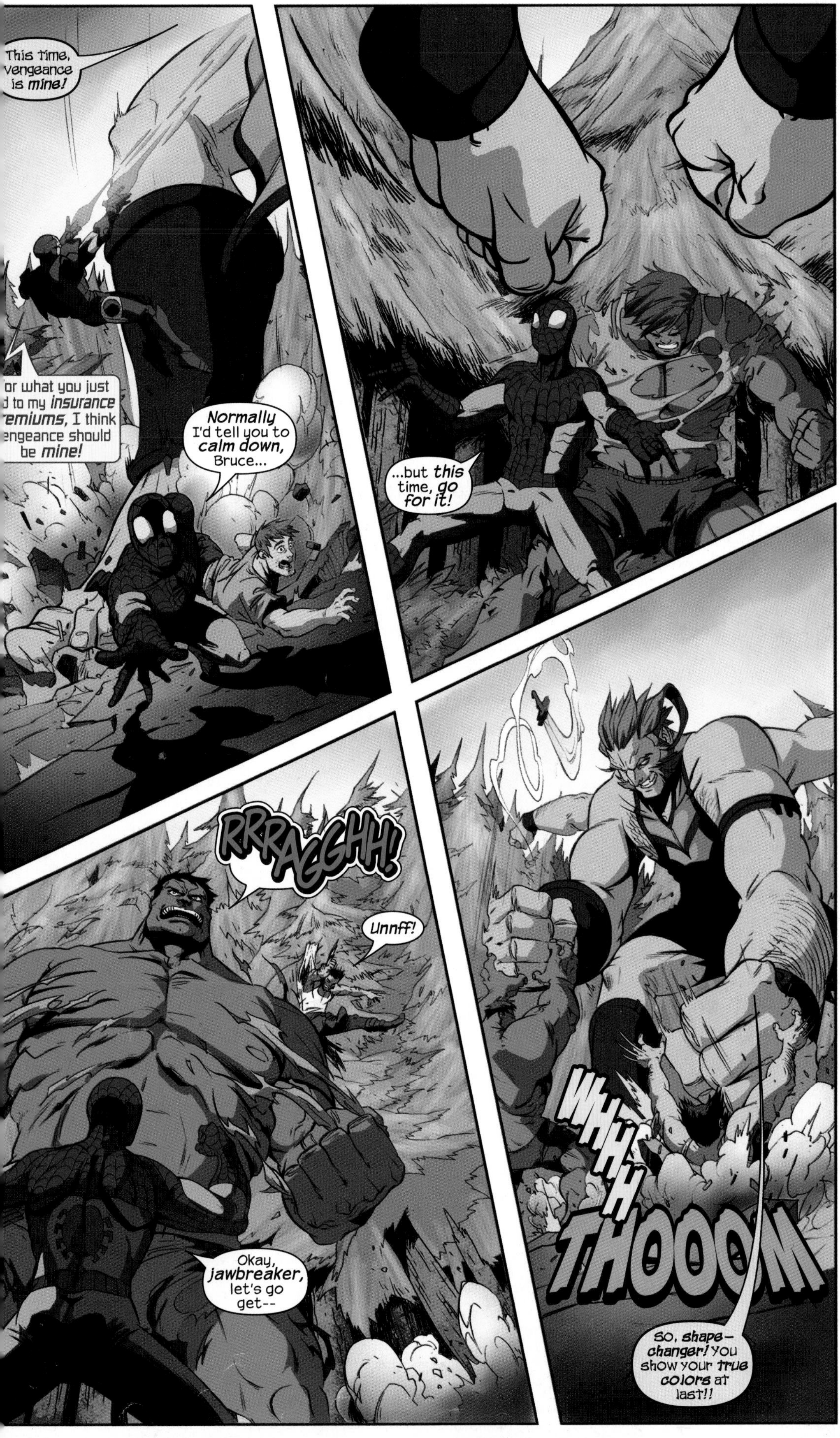

This time, vengeance is *mine!*
or what you just d to my *insurance remiums,* I think engeance should be *mine!*
Normally I'd tell you to *calm down,* Bruce...
...but *this* time, *go for it!*
RRRAGGHH!
Unnff!
Okay, *jawbreaker,* let's go get--
WHHHH
THOOOM
So, *shape-changer!* You show your *true colors* at last!!

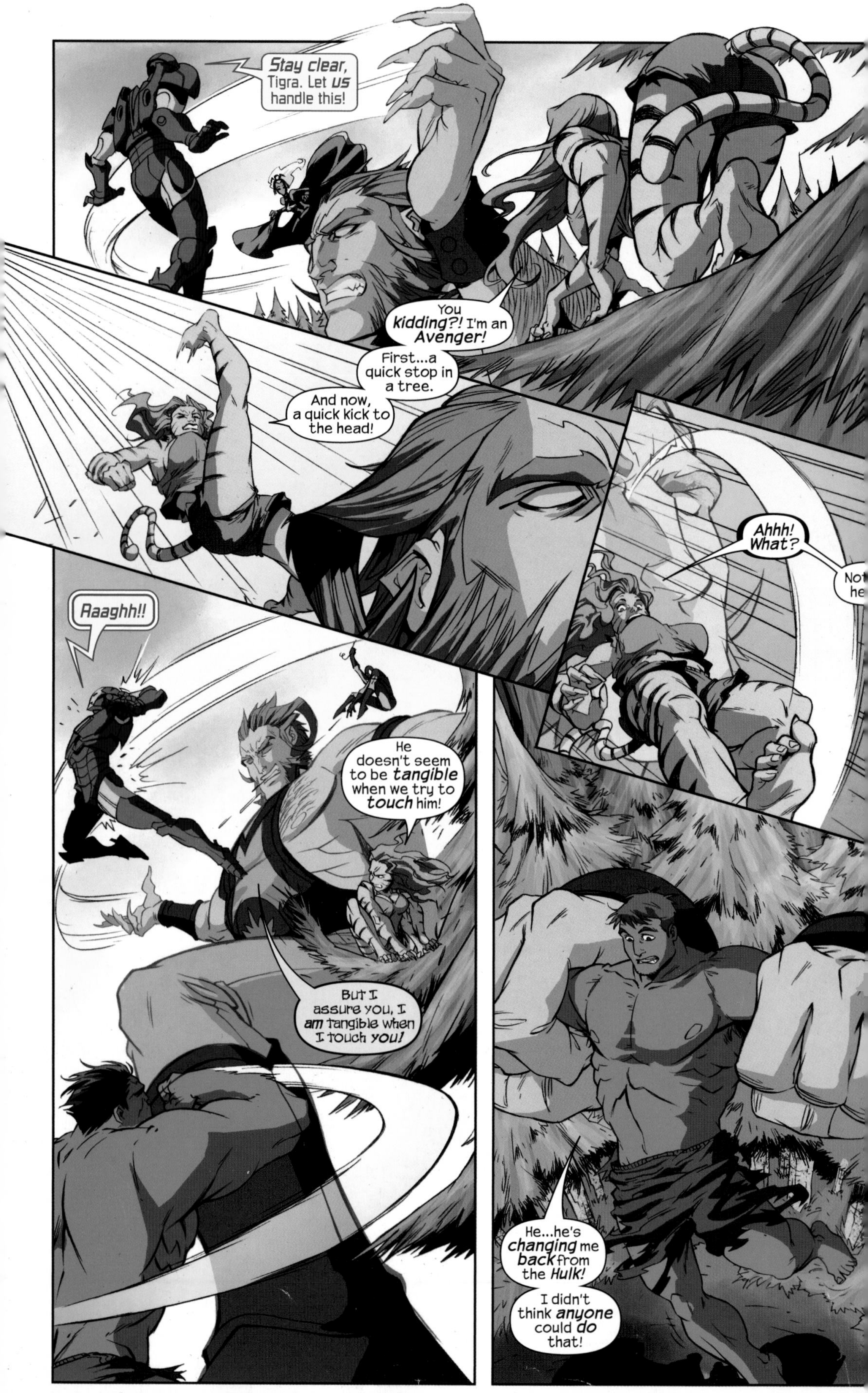
Stay clear, Tigra. Let US handle this!
You kidding?! I'm an Avenger!
First...a quick stop in a tree.
And now, a quick kick to the head!
Ahhh! What?
Raaghh!!
He doesn't seem to be tangible when we try to touch him!
But I assure you, I am tangible when I touch you!
He...he's changing me back from the Hulk!
I didn't think anyone could do that!

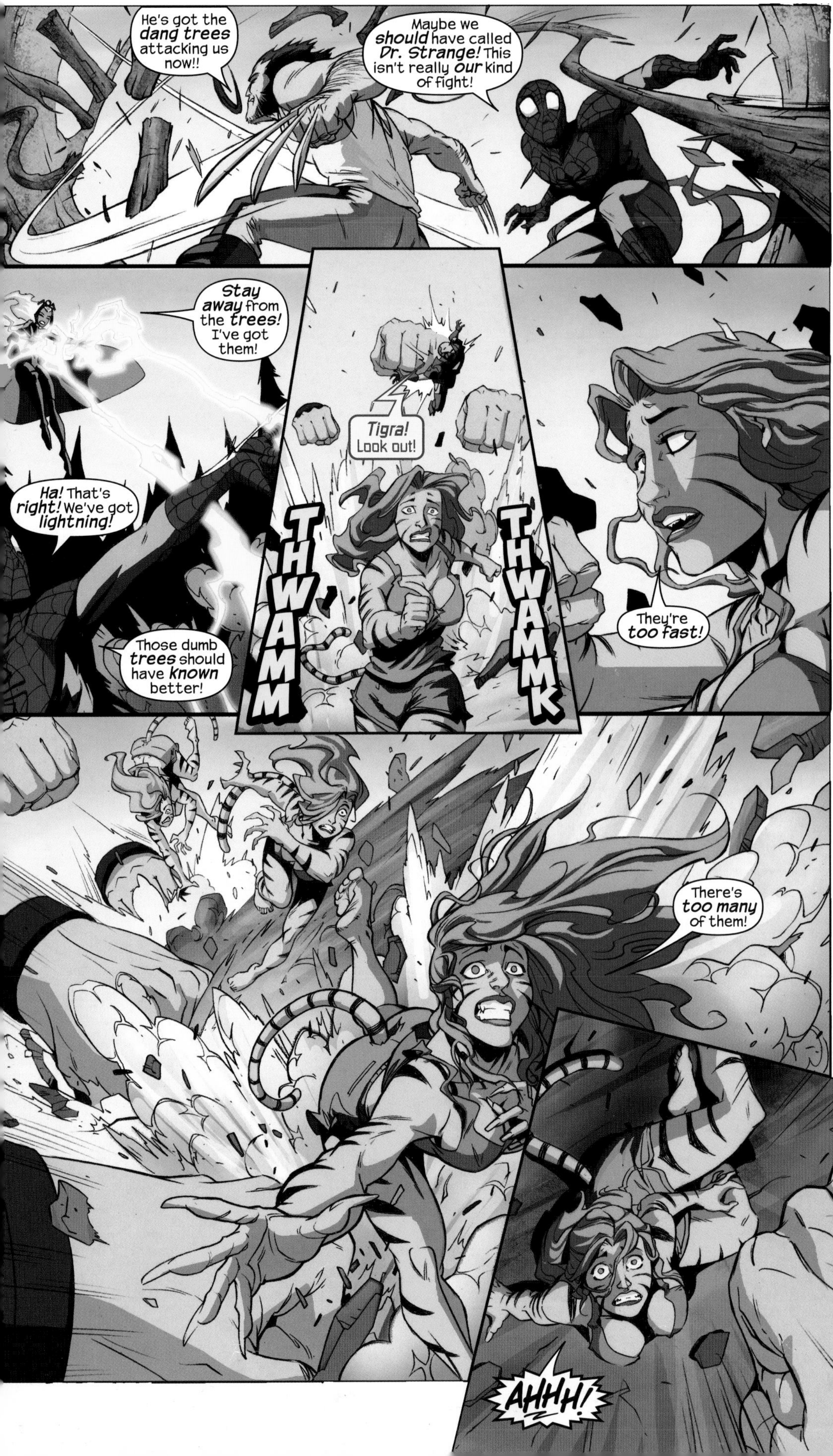
He's got the dang trees attacking us now!!
Maybe we should have called Dr. Strange! This isn't really our kind of fight!
Stay away from the trees! I've got them!
Ha! That's right! We've got lightning!
Those dumb trees should have known better!
Tigra! Look out!
THWAMM
THWAMMK
They're too fast!
There's too many of them!
AHHH!

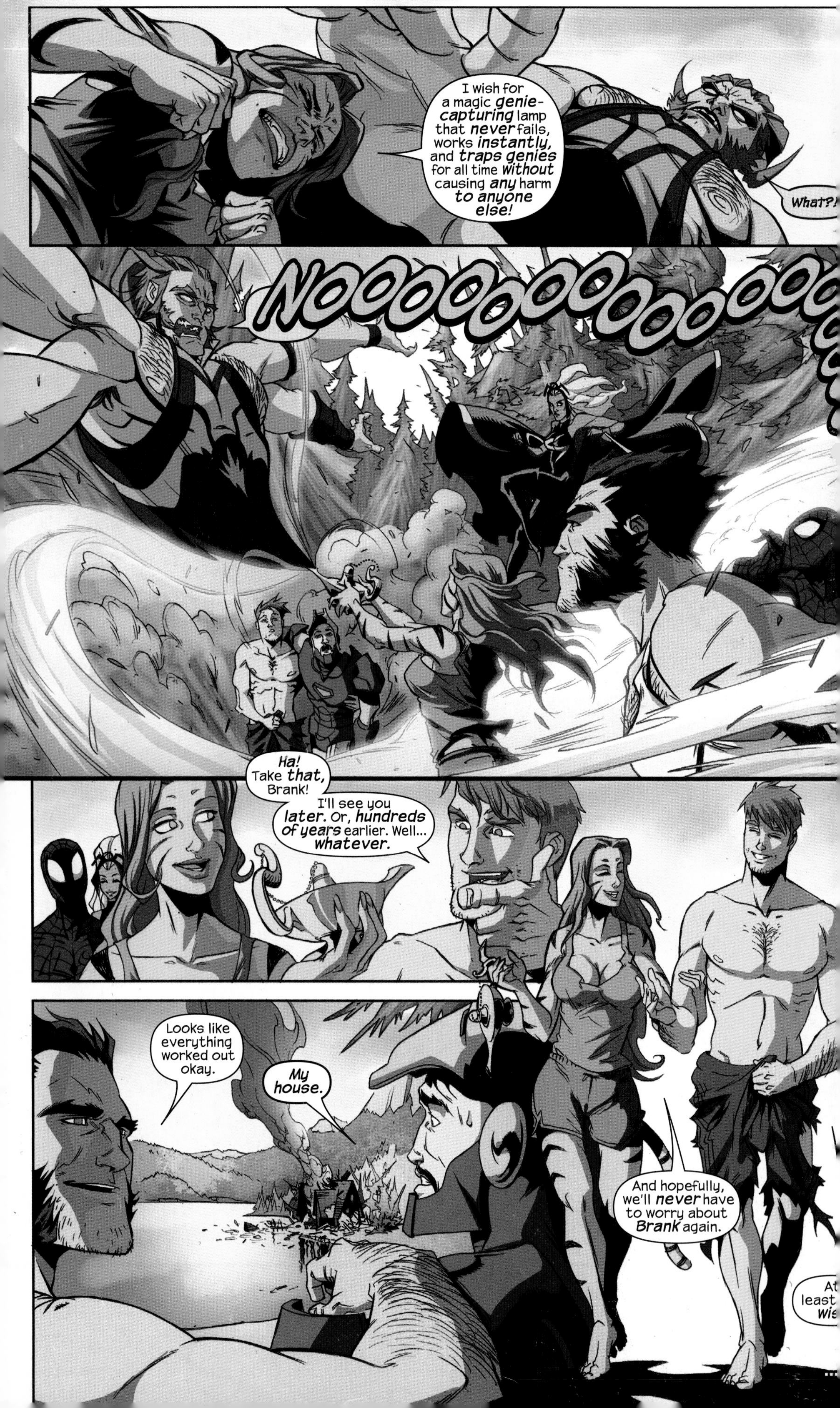
I wish for a magic genie-capturing lamp that never fails, works instantly, and traps genies for all time without causing any harm to anyone else!
What?!
NOOOOOOOOOOOOOO
Ha! Take that, Brank!
I'll see you later. Or, hundreds of years earlier. Well... whatever.
Looks like everything worked out okay.
My house.
And hopefully, we'll never have to worry about Brank again.